This Book Belongs To

To all my first grade students who are starting to read non-fiction - P.L.

Me on the Page Publishing
Copyright © 2018 Phelicia Lang

ISBN-13: 978-0-578-42980-9

Illustrations Copyright © Phelicia Lang

Book Design by Cassandra Bowen, Uzuri Designs
http://uzuridesignsbooks.com

Tay

By Phelicia Lang

Book 6

AN EARLY
READER SERIES

Illustrated by
Samanta Veliz

Reading Tips

Dear Family,

Learning to read non-fiction/informational text is very different from reading stories from cover to cover. Reading to learn information will require your child to understand the layout of the text, the meaning of the symbols and features, as well as finding out where to find key information. It's very much like reading a map; you must understand the keys and symbols.

'Tay goes to the Zoo' is an excellent choice to introduce fiction text features. It includes captions and photographs; two non-fiction features.

Now!, put on your safari hat, and get your binoculars! It's time to learn about some zoo animals! Be sure to ask your reader: "What do you notice?"

Enjoy the tour!!

Phelicia Lang

If your child gets stuck on a word...

Look at the picture	
Touch each letter and say its sound slowly	**bag**
Go back and re-read	
Skip the word and come back to it	**bag** and
Go back and read it again	

Remember to always think...

- **Does my word make sense?**
- **Does my word look right?**
- **Does my word sound right?**

Tay
Goes to the
Zoo

Welcome to the
Zoo

This is Tay.

He is very smart.

He likes to read about animals.

Today is Tay's birthday. His parents have a suprise for him.

Tay and his family
will go on a train.
Where are they going?

Is it the library?

The train stops.

Is it the kids park?

They do not get off.
Where areTay and
his family going?

Tay says, "I know, where we're going. We're going to the game!".

The train stops and they get on a bus.

Tays sees his friends on the bus!! This is a big surprise???

Where could they be going?

They arrive at the
zoo and buy tickets.

What animals will
they see first?

Tay and his friends
play the I spy game!

This animal likes to bathe in the sun and it is brown.

What is it?

It is a sun bear!

Sun bears live in the forest and some swamps.

This animal has a very, very long neck.

What is it?

It is a giraffe.

They have long necks and legs.

This animal is pink and has very long legs.

What is it?

It is a flamingo!

Flamingos have webbed feet like a duck.

This animal looks like a squirrel, but it is a monkey.

What is it?

It is a
squirrel
monkey!

The squirrel monkey's tail is longer than its body. Their bodies are as long as a ruler.

This animal has orange fur and black stripes.

What is it?

It is a tiger.

Tigers can hear very well.

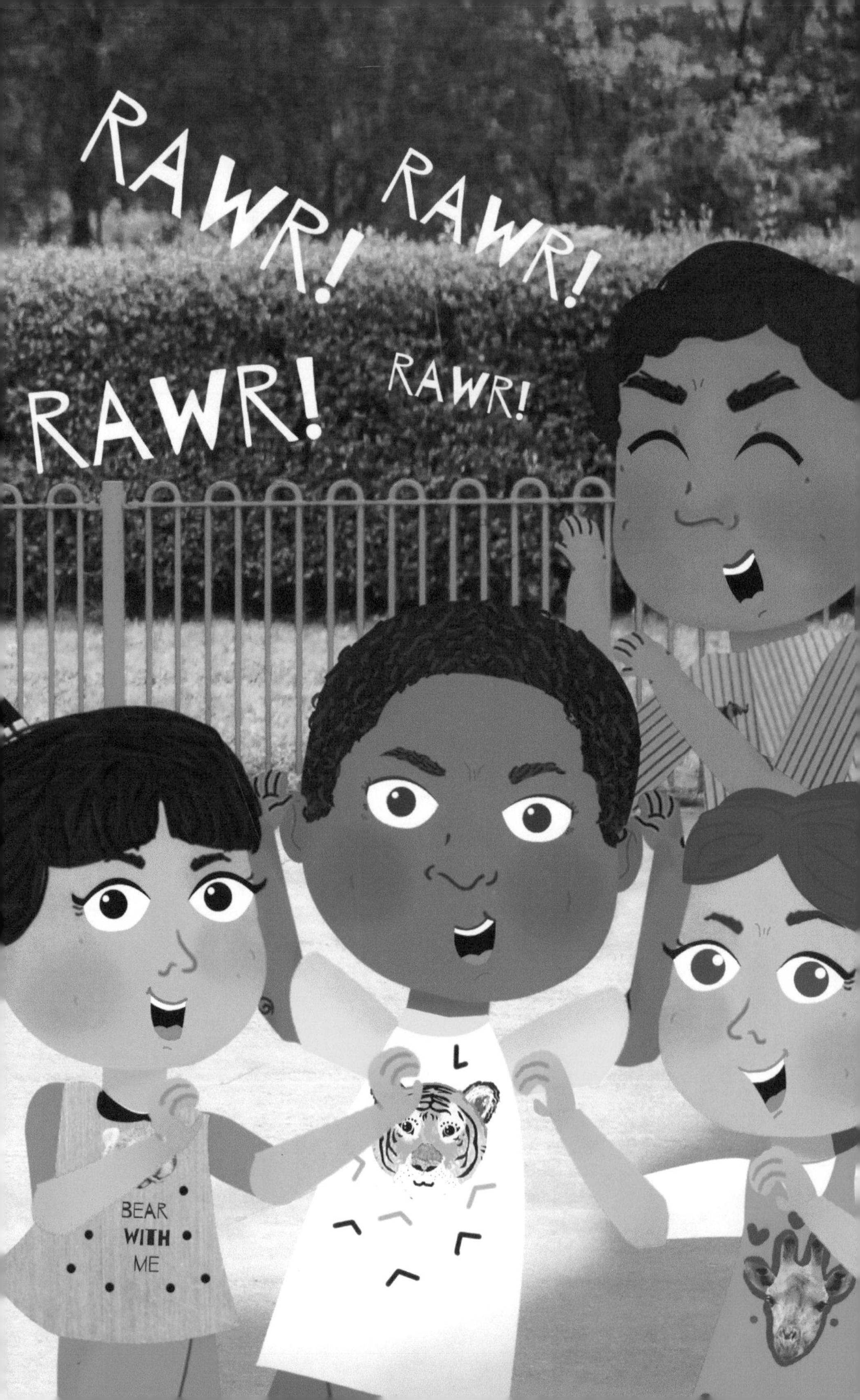
RAWR!
RAWR!
RAWR!
RAWR!
BEAR WITH ME

Tay's and his friends growl like a tiger.

It's time to have
lunch and eat cake!

Tay's friends sing
happy birthday to him.

It is time to go home.

Tay and his friends wave goodbye to the animals.

They had a fun day at the zoo.

About the Author

Phelicia is a loving wife to Tony, mother to four wonderful children and a precious grandson. They have all inspired her journey to find good books to reflect their lives and interests.

As a Reading Specialist she's passionate about finding the right books to help readers connect to stories they love and books that reflect the readers.

Dreaming big dreams and using those dreams and gifts to help others, is the message she shares with her students.

When she's not creating on her computer she can be found Dreaming Big Dreams, reading and shopping.